ANNA WRIGHT was born and raised deep in the Scottish countryside of Dumfriesshire, near a tiny village called Tynron. From a farming family, she grew up with animals all around her and, living as she did in the remote countryside, she learned to become creative in her spare time.

Anna studied at Edinburgh College of Art, where initially she wanted to pursue her interest in costume and textiles, but soon fell in love with illustration. Over the years she has built up a business selling her art and designs, operating from both Edinburgh and London. Anna's work has been featured in *House & Garden*, *Country Life*, and *Artists & Illustrators*. You can find Anna at **www.annawright.co.uk** and on Instagram: **@annawrightillustration**

THE TWELVE DAYS OF CHRISTMAS

ILLUSTRATED BY

Anna Wright

ff

FABER & FABER

On the **first** day of Christmas,
my true love sent to me –
A partridge in a pear tree.

On the **second** day of Christmas,
my true love sent to me –
Two turtle doves,
And a partridge in a pear tree.

On the **third** day of Christmas,
my true love sent to me –
Three French hens,
Two turtle doves,
And a partridge in a pear tree.

On the fourth day of Christmas,
my true love sent to me –
Four calling birds,
Three French hens,
Two turtle doves,
And a partridge in a pear tree.

O n the **fifth** day of Christmas,
my true love sent to me –
Five gold rings,
Four calling birds,
Three French hens,
Two turtle doves,
And a partridge in a pear tree.

O n the **sixth** day of Christmas,
my true love sent to me –
Six geese a-laying,
Five gold rings,
Four calling birds,
Three French hens,
Two turtle doves,
And a partridge in a pear tree.

On the seventh day of Christmas,
my true love sent to me –
Seven swans a-swimming,
Six geese a-laying,
Five gold rings,
Four calling birds,
Three French hens,
Two turtle doves,
And a partridge in a pear tree.

On the eighth day of Christmas,
my true love sent to me –
Eight maids a-milking,
Seven swans a-swimming,
Six geese a-laying,
Five gold rings,
Four calling birds,
Three French hens,
Two turtle doves,
And a partridge in a pear tree.

On the **ninth** day of Christmas,
my true love sent to me –
Nine ladies dancing,
Eight maids a-milking,
Seven swans a-swimming,
Six geese a-laying,
Five gold rings,
Four calling birds,
Three French hens,
Two turtle doves,
And a partridge in a pear tree.

On the **tenth** day of Christmas,
my true love sent to me –
Ten lords a-leaping,
Nine ladies dancing,
Eight maids a-milking,
Seven swans a-swimming,
Six geese a-laying,
Five gold rings,
Four calling birds,
Three French hens,
Two turtle doves,
And a partridge in a pear tree.

On the **eleventh** day of Christmas,
my true love sent to me –
Eleven pipers piping,
Ten lords a-leaping,
Nine ladies dancing,
Eight maids a-milking,
Seven swans a-swimming,
Six geese a-laying,
Five gold rings,
Four calling birds,
Three French hens,
Two turtle doves,
And a partridge in a pear tree.

On the twelfth day of Christmas,
my true love sent to me –
Twelve drummers
                drumming,
Eleven pipers piping,
Ten lords a-leaping,
Nine ladies dancing,
Eight maids a-milking,
Seven swans a-swimming,
Six geese a-laying,
Five gold rings,
Four calling birds,
Three French hens,
Two turtle doves,
And a partridge in a pear tree.